The Everyday Life Bible: Notes & Commentary by Joyce Meyer. First Edition:
Faith Words. New York, NY 2020. Print.
https://www.youversion.com/apps/New International Version
https://www.youversion.com/apps/New King James Version
https://www.youversion.com/apps/King James Version
https://www.youversion.com/apps/Message Version

LWI Publishing Services

Contact info:
info@joanldavislifecoaching.com
www.joanldavislifecoaching.com

Printed in the United States of America
First Printing: March 2023

≫ Table of Contents

Letter to Reverend Nobodies and "No Names"

Introduction

≫ Table of Contents

Letter to the "Reverend Nobodies" and to the "No Names."

I greet each of you with the Joy and Love of Jesus Christ.

I want you to know how wonderful and beautiful you are. For you, "Reverend Nobodies" and all other "No Names", you were Created by the One who sees us in His Own Image.

The Shadows many of us had to undertake, were not from our Heavenly Father, but those shadows came from the ones who did not recognize who we were, while in their midst. Being part of and attending many meetings, entering into rooms being overlooked. Not recognized because they could not see you beyond the scars of the shadows.

Facing shadows such as depression, loneliness, anxiety, stress, losing hope, unable to trust, all these shadows were in place due to the ones who would not see past your worth.

Reverend Nobody is the voice not only for herself but for all of the "Reverend Nobodies" and "No Names" who had to sit in their shadows thinking there was no hope, no way out, because societies made it feel that way.

However, there is freedom for us, there is peace for us, there is joy for us, there is strength for us, there is love for us, there is breakthrough for us, there are rewards for us, there is victory for us, there are achievements and there are accomplishments for us. This list goes on and on not because I say so but because God says so. There are Scriptures that let us know that Our Heavenly Father is with us and that no matter what we face, He will never leave us nor forsake us.

In every chapter, you will find Scriptures to let you know that our shadows do not define who we are. While we were not being recognized by humankind as worthy to be a part of, we were already recognized by the One who Created you and me, all the "Reverend Nobodies" and all the "No Names."

The Scriptures tell us of many "No Names" in the Bible who were never recognized or accepted in the community because the ones who were in charge did not find them worthy; however, the Word tells us differently. For the Bible tells us that The Father, chose all of the "No Names" to be His Ambassadors and they did the work of their Father. In the same way, today, in our time, God is choosing us, the Reverend Nobodies and the "No Names" to be His, Our Heavenly Father's, Ambassadors.

Now my Reverend Nobodies and my "No Names", let us not allow our shadows to keep us from the promises which Our Father has for us. Know that in our shadows God is with you, and with us. According to His Words through the prophets Isaiah and Jeremiah. The prophet Isaiah 41:10; "So do not fear, for I am with you; do not be dismayed, for I am your God. I will strengthen you and help you; I will uphold you with my righteous right hand." The prophet Jeremiah 29:11; "For I know the plans I have for you, "declares the Lord," plans to prosper you and not to harm you, plans to give you hope and a future."

May the Lord bless you and keep you now and always. Now, my fellow "Reverend Nobodies" and "No Names" let us walk in our anointing for the journey.

Reverend Nobody

INTRODUCTION

How many times have you been criticized without the proper information especially when you know that God called you to the ministry of pastoral. Even through your repentance and having your past wiped away by God, there are those that deem you unworthy and continue to criticize and offer up questions like; Are you are on the path that God called you to? Why would God call you? Are you sure you heard Him correctly? Reverend Nobody will give you a deep look inside of not only her personal journey but also the journey of the women in the Bible, who, had "No names," yet God used them to be His ambassadors, His messengers, His helpers, the list goes on and on.

This book was not only written for Reverend Nobody. It is written to be the voice for the many "Nobodies" that society has written off from answering their own calling in becoming the ambassadors God ordained them to fulfill.

Reverend Nobody was written for the women who know that God called them to be His ambassadors, but because of your past, you may believe you do not fit "the mold". You look at the others called and struggle because you are not a part of their clicks - meaning you are not in their special groups, you do not smell like them, you do not look like them, and you do not dress like them, and they have declared you as a "Nobody". Let me be the first to tell you that God wants you to know that He did not create you to fit in, you were created to be set apart. You are His anointed. Only He can declare who you are, whose you are, and the only One that can order your step for only He knows the plans He has for you.

Reverend Nobody was created to capture the ones, who still are without a name because God has a plan, He has predestinated you to be a part of His Kingdom Building. This book will help us to realize and understand that the same way they attempt to write us off is the same way they claimed Jesus was a "Nobody" because He was not born into royalty, and His clothing was not lined with gold. Reverend Nobody will help us to see the brighter outcome and really look at the assignments that His Father sent Him to overcome.

Yes, I too, was looked upon as a "Nobody," but it is the favor of God, His Grace, and His Mercy that proved them wrong and is still proving them wrong. And today I, Joan L Davis, "Reverend Nobody", after all I have been through, am still standing in the promises God has for me, not as the "Reverend Nobody" they wanted me to be, but as the "Reverend Somebody" God created me to be.

I declare and decree for all who may have been overlooked and seen as that "Nobody" you will not accept the name. You will turn your ears to the only One that can define you. You will start believing that you are "Somebody" for God says you are according to His Word by the prophet **Jeremiah 29:11**; *"For I know the plans I have for you," declares the Lord, "plans to prosper you and not to harm you, plans to give you hope and a future" (NIV).*

Now let's take the journey in finding your true identity given to you by Our Heavenly Father.

"Before I formed you in the womb
I knew you, before you were born I
set you apart; I appointed you as a
prophet to the nations"

JEREMIAH 1:5

CHAPTER ONE
Who is Reverend Nobody?

Hiding behind all the unkind words spoken over her life by many, Reverend Nobody had to stand on her own. Standing on her own did not mean Reverend Nobody was or had been forgotten or that she was in by herself. No, it meant God shielded her so that He could mold, equip, and empower Reverend Nobody for the journey He had prepared for His daughter.

In the eyes of Reverend Nobody, she may have thought that she was by herself, but she was getting ready to understand that the favor of God was with and within her. She was never alone, for her greatest protector is the One who entrusts her to be His vessel in writing what He has to say concerning Reverend Nobody. For He is The Creator, The Father, The One who knows that He had to keep her hidden from the knowns and the unknowns until it was time.

Reverend Nobody was never meant to be in front or used to be a showcase. Even though to Reverend Nobody, it seemed she was never recognized, she had to accept who God wanted her to be. For God had greater plans for Reverend Nobody. Plans that no humankind could imagine or begin to understand. Why Reverend Nobody, would be their question.

For it was easy to keep looking at who Reverend Nobody was through natural eyes, but it was another thing to look from your spiritual eyes. The only way you were able to see through your spiritual eyes, was to have a deep intimate personal relationship with the Father. Only then would you understand that she was being protected by her true Creator.

It is easy to be overlooked by the ones who just cannot seem to see past your look. All they see is that you are not part of their social group. Dare I say, they didn't deem me worthy enough to be a part of their world. It was easy to think that something was wrong with me, no matter what I brought or contributed to their conversations. I was never accepted. The crazy thing was when someone else presented the same input to the conversation, it was found to be acceptable and many praises were given to that individual or individuals. Their name or names were announced at meetings, and services but never Reverend Nobody.

Nothing seemed to be of a good fit for Reverend Nobody, leaving her to dwell in the loneliness of her journey. But it was not her will, but the Will of The Heavenly Father who was keeping her in His arms. You may be asking why Reverend Nobody was so shielded by God, but it is not for her to defend or explain such protection for God is the One who ordained her to be His child.

He guarded His daughter, from the ones who would cast their own opinion and make their own judgment against Reverend Nobody. It is easy to make decisions about Reverend Nobody when all you see is that she does not fit, but in God's eyes, Reverend Nobody is not seen that way. For like Joseph, David, Moses, the Woman at the Well, the Woman healed by a touch, and the Samaritan Woman, they did not fit into the group, yet God used them so that His glory could be revealed.

While the question still remains, "Who is Reverend Nobody?" It is not for you to know who Reverend Nobody is by name and why all these things happened, but it is to know the One who works through her so you can come to know more about Him. The One who created her in His Own Image, wonderfully made in the eyes and beauty of her Father, the One who predestined the plans of craftsmanship for His purpose. She was created with a purpose and a promise given to her by The Father.

"For I know the plans I have for you," declares the Lord, "plans to prosper you and not to harm you, plans to give you hope and a future"

Jeremiah 29:11

CHAPTER TWO
The Journey of Reverend Nobody

The Journey of Reverend Nobody is still a mystery to many. Leaving those who are still questioning, in a space of trying to figure out how. How can all this happen to someone who does not have a well-known family legacy, does not own a home, be an unmarried mother of five, and does not have a 6-figure job? How is it possible for this individual a "Reverend Nobody," to be so well-maintained and established in her journey?

Reverend Nobody does not owe her journey to anyone other than the One who created her and the One who opened every door that humankind wanted to keep closed on her. No, Reverend Nobody, was never alone, for I, The Father was always with her. In all your own disbelief, you questioned her. Asking how did all this happen for her? How did someone who is not well-known, with no strong family ties in the community get there? How was it possible for her to travel to the Holy Land? How can Reverend Nobody whom we have cast out from the programs and who struggles with writing become an author? How did Reverend Nobody get elected at the height of the pandemic to be ordained, and how did she move through the process so rapidly? How did Reverend Nobody host and have her first Women's Conference?

All these questions you have asked of My daughter, you were asking them of Me, Who I AM. And in the same way, you have asked similar questions about My Son, Jesus Christ when He was carrying the duty of His Father.

Some of you question her worthiness of being in the Holy Land, feeling you were more worthy. Why it is so important to know how and why she went on this trip? Do you know the God she serves? Are you in relationship with the God she trusts? The God she has faith in? The God she knows who will provide all her needs? Do you know the God she has surrendered all to? Not some things but ALL things. Reverend Nobody knows Me and I rewarded her. I, The Father made the way for My daughter to go to the place where it all started. Yes, the place I sent My Son to fulfill His purpose. Yes, the place He experienced all that His Father needed Him to experience before the start of His Ministry. Yes, it is the same place I, The Father sent My daughter, Reverend Nobody to experience before she started her Ministry journey in fulfilling all that her Father has for her to do.

While there, I, The Father and My daughter, Reverend Nobody spent time in Solitude. My daughter was sent to the Holy Land to experience the times My Son spent with Me. It is at those moments I, The Father was preparing My daughter. I, The Father, anointed, equipped, and empowered My daughter for the journey in which I have ordained her according to the plans I, The Father have for her.

When you became jealous and rejected her, you were saying I, The Father your God was not real. When you overlooked her, you were saying, I, The Father cannot do the impossible because you deemed her impossible. When you hurt her, you hurt me.

You have questioned everything I had Reverend Nobody do in My Name. You have yet to understand the power of your Heavenly Father. Reverend Nobody has not held herself back from Me. You claim you see Me in her but you couldn't possibly or you wouldn't have overlooked her. You have criticized her movement not realizing she was moving according to My Word which means you were criticizing Me. For I, The Father knows the plans I have and have preordained Reverend Nobody to achieve. I have taken Reverend Nobody out of a place that many of you have tried to lock her in, while pouring the most unforgiving words of lies out of your mouths. My Divine Words speak of the ones who will come in My Name. My Word says, "He who has eyes to see will see and he who has ears to hear, let him hear. Everyone who has eyes will not see, not because they are unable but because they do not want to."

At no time have you sought I, The Father about My daughter, before speaking words of hurt. All this time if you had sought Me, you would have known that I, The Father was in the control of Reverend Nobody's journey. I was the one that provided her the strength to endure your words of doubt and discouragement. I called her author, you declared her wordless, I called her preacher, you defined her mute, I called her worthy, you shouted from the rooftops worthless. Let it be known that your words fell on barren soil and will never take root.

I, The Father rewarded My daughter for her faithfulness and obedient humility in doing her Father's work. I AM the One who allowed Reverend Nobody to make history. Many of you struggle to accept her reward but it is not for you to accept. My Word states you are to rejoice with one another and not be envious. If you knew Me you would know My Word and you would desire to be obedient to it.

"*Trust in the Lord with all your heart and lean not on your own understanding; in all your ways submit to him, and he will make your paths straight*"

Proverbs 3:5-6

CHAPTER THREE

When no one sees you for your worth?

God said, "*No one needs to see your worth Reverend Nobody because you were a presentation of Who I AM. They did not see My Son's worth, with all the miracles He performed they still questioned and wondered who He was. For He was only a carpenter's son. Who was He to be able to perform such miracles, they wondered. There are so many Reverend Nobodies out there enduring the shunning just like the woman with the issue of the blood. Others who endure the judgment like the adulterous woman. The ones who are considered too old like Sarah, too wayward like Rahab but yet God never overlooked them. Not only did God see them, but He also used them for His glory and His kingdom.*

The same way I, The Father sent My Son to represent Me is the same way I send My daughter Reverend Nobody to represent Me. Many of you get caught up trying to figure out why this person and not you. As The Father, I trust her the same way I have trusted My Son. I trusted that they would not take credit for what I, The Father have done and Am doing through them. I long for my children to stop looking at one another and coveting what I, the Father, give.

Many of you take the credit for yourself or give it to someone who won't even acknowledge who I AM. That is why you do not acknowledge or give credit to Reverend Nobody because she is not about taking credit, she going to give the credit to The Father.

I have known each of you and knew what you would do to her. I shielded Reverend Nobody from all of your selfish actions because nothing about it was representing Who I AM. It was all for your praise. The times she hurt, I allowed her to see who you were and whom you were not representing so she could understand her separation stage. You believed you were looking in Reverend Nobody's face, when in fact, you were looking directly into My face and treating Me in those unkindly ways. I have seen you on the phone and heard you talking about Me. Yes, Me, the one you declare you love, your Heavenly Father. Had you paid attention to my Word, you would have noticed, I said, what you do to the least of them you do to Me.

Reverend Nobody represents Who I AM, for it is I who lives, operates, moves, speaks, loves, and walks through My daughter. She is a representation of who I AM. When you hurt her with your unkind words, yes you were hurting Me. When you push her out yes you were pushing Me out. I shield her from all your ways and that is why she is Reverend Nobody. I continue to shield her from your ways. Reverend Nobody does not have to justify who she is because I have already done this before she was found in her mother's womb.

99

"And I will do whatever you ask in my Name, so that the Father may be glorified in the Son. Your may ask me for anything in my Name and I will do it"

John 14:13-14

CHAPTER FOUR

Something about the Name Jesus in those moments

My people were foretold of My coming Son, but they did not accept the upcoming news from My prophet Isaiah. I had told of Him so that when the time came they would have been welcoming and understanding of Who He was and why He was sent. But many of My people did the opposite. I sent My Son to fulfill the promise I made to Abraham, Isaac, and Jacob, the promise of not bringing judgment as I had during the time of Noah. Instructing Noah to build the Ark and gather together all the livestock and his families, I sent a Mighty destruction upon the land, because of My people's disobedience. After the 40 days of rain I, Your God, sent a peace offering in the symbol of a rainbow. Symbolizing My promise to never bring this level of judgement on the land. I, Your God made a covenant with You, My people. In this New Covenant is where My Son became part of the fulfillment. Yet you still did not accept or want to accept Who He was. My Son, Jesus, was sent by Me to do His Father's work. A work that My Son journeyed through and fulfilled when He went to the cross as part of the atonement to carry all of your sins and burdens and leave them there. However, throughout all His work, miracles, healing, preaching, teaching, crucifying, and rising from the dead, many of you still do not understand the Name of My Son, Jesus, and the power you have when you call on His Name. A name I have given to My Son when He was sent from Heaven to be borne by My Chosen vessel and given the name that He should carry, that name is Jesus, Son of the living God. There is power in the Name of Jesus. There is anointing in the Name of Jesus. There is victory in the Name of Jesus. There is breakthrough in the Name of Jesus. There is deliverance in the Name of Jesus. Speak the Name of My Son and watch the power of The Father.

My daughter, Reverend Nobody, knows the Name of My Son, Jesus. She speaks and calls His Name. Reverend Nobody knew the personal relationship she needed to have with My Son and she has that relationship with Him. Through My daughter's relationship with My Son, I have anointed her with the power and the authority when she calls and speaks of His Name, Jesus. Every demonic jealousy, witchcraft, envy, lying lips, everything that Satan puts in her way, will have, to take flight. My daughter has received the favor of I, The Father, of I, The Son, Jesus, and of I, The Holy Spirit. When you understand who I AM through my Son, Jesus then you will understand who Revered Nobody is to Me.

66

"So do not fear, for I am with you; do not be dismayed, for I am your God. I will strengthen you and help you; I will uphold with my righteous right hand"

99

Isaiah 41:10

CHAPTER FIVE

How to get over when you are overlooked?

Being overlooked in anything can be a difficult experience, especially when you are available for the task at hand. But The Father wants you to know the same way Judas sold His Son Jesus for worldly gain, is the same way there are Judas' today who overlooked Reverend Nobody just for worldly gain in the form of praise, accolades, money, etc. However, My Son still showed him mercy and broke bread with him realizing it was all a part of His Father's plan. In the same way, my daughter sits among her Judas' showing them mercy and serving them knowing it all is all a part of her Father's plan. The reason why is that both were and are representations of who I AM in them. For I, the Father, sent them both to be among you, and in your own selfish ways of taking praises for yourselves and not giving Me the glory, you were unable to see Me in them. You were so busy placing yourselves in front of Me. I have Reverend Nobody sitting with you in some of your meetings, because you did not know who she was, as you looked past her to address everyone else, you didn't even realize you were overlooking Me. I had to have Reverend Nobody hidden so that I could reveal to you that I have sent Reverend Nobody to present Me. I have ordained Reverend Nobody to be My prophet over nations, to tear down and to rebuild to declare in My Name. I had to hide Reverend Nobody for her safety because you were still not open to Me assigning My Own prophets to be among you. You are still not open to hearing direct messages from Me. You shut your eyes and closed to ears because you did not want to receive the message that I had for you from Reverend Nobody. You still continue to question the one I sent to be among you. You use your judgment of her past to justify how you treat her. You place her in a box I never created for her, as if it is your right. I have placed Reverend Nobody to study among you and you find it in her journey to disclaim her because she did write "perfectly" like you. She did not code all the theologians like you. But you claim you sought Me to know her heart. You did not. It is time for you to seek and check the attitude of your own heart. My Word says you will know Me if you seek Me, you will know the ones who represent Me if you seek Me. Reverend Nobody did not fit into your class, she was not part of the organizations that you have formed and for that, you place her on the outside. I had to take Reverend Nobody into the wilderness to be guarded against many of you who were out to destroy her. Reverend Nobody had to experience some experiences so that she would see how you would treat Me. Reverend Nobody was never by herself in those wilderness moments, for I had The Holy Spirit with her, to comfort and guide her. She had My Son to intercede for her strength, when you had beaten her down, without no caring thoughts. She had Me who continued to shield her from the hands who want to break her. I have also placed some of my servants whom I trust that will guard her. She will not have to pull away from you For I, The Father, will pull you away from her.

I know all who did and what was done to My Servant, Reverend Nobody. I AM not here to call out your names. Nor have I allowed Reverend Nobody to call you out by name or acknowledge what you have done. My Word says, there is an appointed time for everything. Reverend Nobody is not here to justify herself to the ones who closed their eyes or wonder why her.

Many did not accept My Son when I sent Him to do His Father's business. So it is not surprising you are not accepting of My daughter whom I have sent among you in this time to do her Father's business. After all the years, My Son has fulfilled His Father's Will, but you still think that it is not possible that The Father would send another. Or rather, you believe that the one I send should fit a mold according to the world. If you are My child, then you are no longer of this world. So why do you measure my daughter against the world's standards of worthiness?

It may be hard for you to understand that Reverend Nobody was chosen by Me, to be My representative in this century, but it is so. It is I Who has sent Reverend Nobody to fulfill my Works. I have equipped, trained, empowered, and gifted her with the tools to do My Will.

I have placed My daughter in your presence because I have empowered her with all the knowledge for your location but you have chosen to overlook My Presence and you decided to place the ones I did not assign in positions I did not create and then you wondered why your efforts were to no avail. You made your decision without seeking Me, The Father. You made selfish decisions in trying to block Reverend Nobody. You cannot stop me from completing the plans that I have. My plans remain, my promises stand so all you have done is delay what I have put in place.

"For those who find me find life and receive favor from the Lord"

CHAPTER SIX

His Grace and His Mercy

For I know the plans I have in store for Reverend Nobody. I took her from her hometown and in Me, through Me, and by Me, Reverend Nobody has found great favor in her Heavenly Father. For it was My Grace and My Mercy that when you were planning a trap for Reverend Nobody, I hid her. Yes, many of you cowardly hid as you set traps and plans to defeat her. In those plots, I had to show Reverend Nobody visions and dreams of all her attackers. I also let My daughter know it was not for her to confront her attackers, but it was for her Father to fight her battles. You did not see Reverend Nobody as qualified in your eyes, but she was already qualified before she was formed in her mother's womb.

Reverend Nobody did not have to speak to defend herself for it is I, The Father who speaks on her behalf. Yes, in some of those times, I have chosen the ones who will speak on her behalf. The ones I know who would not take credit for themselves and like my daughter have surrendered all to me. They are obedient to my Word. Reverend Nobody has found great favor in Me, I have chosen and instructed her to be My scribe in sharing with many who are still questioning who Reverend Nobody is. It is through My Grace and My Mercy, Reverend Nobody has found such blessings in Me. Such anointing in Me. It is through Me that Reverend Nobody can stand in any audience and empower others to know the plans I have for them.

It is through Me that Reverend Nobody walked among you bold with such authorities to speak to the ones whom I have placed in her path, leaving you questioning, her and Me. It is I, The Father who have given her the authorities and gifted her to speak in My Name. A charge that I have given to Reverend Nobody to love, and to care, and to be among My People. A charge that many of you still choose to ignore. Before you say you don't ignore that charge, look at the way you treat all the Reverend Nobodies I have placed among you.

"You did not choose Me, but I chose you and appointed you so that you might go and bear fruit – fruit that will last – and so that whatever you ask in My Name the Father will give you"

John 15:16

CHAPTER SEVEN
The "No Name" women in the Bible

I, The Father, have Chosen many women without names who have been considered as "No Names" in the Bible whom I have identified to be My Ambassador to serve others. There are a few women that have done great work for Me, in which they were known for their great work without the title of a name associated.

The Shunammite Woman, looking for nothing in return showed kindness to My prophet and his servant. This woman only known as "The Shunammite Woman," in 2 Kings 4:8-10, provided a room and provisions for My servant, Elisha. She served in the position that I wanted her to and showed care to My prophet without asking or seeking self-acknowledgment.

The Canaanite Woman, who accepted her calling to do mission work even in the midst of being rejected by the many around her. My daughter, without a name, did not stop seeking Me. Her not being acknowledged did not stop her from fulfilling the work of what it meant to be persistent to Me, The Father. My daughter, a name as "The Canaanite Woman," Matthew 15:21-28 did not allow her rejectors to prevent her from the position I, The Father, placed her in, to be My Ambassador.

What Reverend Nobody and the other women share in common with one another is their commitment to Me. At some point in their lives, they chose to commit to Me and My Word. Each of them was faced with something and chose obedience over circumstances. They pushed through all of your unkind words, and judgmental come backs toward them. They moved forward despite you trying to steer away from what you believe belonged to you. Your behavior towards My daughters hurt Me. I felt their pain, I heart their cries, I healed their wounds. For in Me, My daughters had to face humiliation, but none of this surprised me, I knew you would do this and prepared them for it. It didn't mean they wouldn't hurt, but it did mean they would continue to stand despite it.

Yes, Reverend Nobody, My daughter the Canaanite Woman, as well as My daughter known as the Woman at the Well they all endured the darts you threw at them with the mean unkind words coming out of your mouths, never wondering or considering that you were speaking to I, The Father.

Although you treated My daughters, the way you thought was right, I, The Father never returned to you those unkind treatments. For, I, The Father still extended to each of you, My Grace and My Mercy. Despite the fact that you had it in your hearts to show such extreme levels of unkindness, My daughter Reverend Nobody cried unto Me to have mercy upon you. Reverend Nobody, the one you did not see worthy, was interceding to Me, The Father on your behalf. For many of you, while you were laying on your sick beds, financially unstable, she was crying out to Me on your behalf. Yet, in your ways, you have never sought or asked for forgiveness. Even when I had Reverend Nobody, without any fault of hers, let you know she forgave you, you still went on your way as if you did nothing wrong.

However, what you did not know, I, The Father was letting you know I, Your Father was giving you another chance. I, The Father, I AM well pleased with My daughters in the same way I, The Father was pleased with My Son, Jesus when I sent Him to earth to face all the humiliation. Because they all did and are doing the Work of their Heavenly Father.

"being confident of this, that he who began a good work in you will carry it on to completion until the day of Christ Jesus"

Philippians 1:6

CHAPTER EIGHT

God still uses the "No Names" for His Glory

My children, why have you spent so much time concerning yourselves with Reverend Nobody's worthiness? All this time you spend worrying rather than seeking Me. You were so busy trying to figure out how to move her out of the way, how to ensure she didn't reach her goals or rather walk in the calling I placed on her life. Not realizing that I, The Father, had placed her in the position to do what I have anointed her to do. All this time you were working against My servant, you were working against Me, Your Father, because I was there with her and I still am. I see what you plot in the dark, I hear what you whisper, I know your thoughts despite the fact that you say you are My child and you surrender to My Word but you do not. For My Word says to love your neighbor as yourself. My Word says if you say you love Me but you hate your brother then you are a liar.

Reverend Nobody did not only surrender to Me by accepting the calling, but she also sacrificed everything, she released everything to Me. You continued to ask why her, I, the Father, say why not her? I have ordained Reverend Nobody and have sent her out in My Name to be among many of you. You are all My children, she is your sister but you treat her like she is your enemy. Many of you are still not willing to accept who she is. For Reverend Nobody does not have that well-known name, according to you. A name that you can give self-praise to, a name that you can associate with some club or organization, a name that you can take credit for. But you are still missing the point, Reverend Nobody is connected to the ultimate Name, the Name above all Names.

This is about your desire for self-praise, you want to worship who and what you want to worship. You want to respect and honor what you want to. You want to elevate who and what you elevate. You want to say you are mine but move like you belong to the world. You want to control until you can no longer control and then you want to call on me to fix what you cannot. You have come into My House and made a mockery it My House and the Ones I have placed in it. When I placed Moses in charge of my people to guide them, it was because I deemed Him worthy not My people. When I made David King, it was because I placed Him in that position not because My people deemed him worthy of the position or the journey.

When you decided that you had the right to attempt to move Reverend Nobody, from the positions I placed her in, you were playing god. You were not only saying that she did not belong there, you were also saying that I did not belong there. In your boldness to state where I could or could not place Reverend Nobody, you were attempting to place Me in a box. I have sent Reverend Nobody to love the ones who have been rejected, the ones who need to be loved, and cared for. I was the One who had Reverend Nobody share with each of you what it meant to trust Me, The Father. However, you were so busy focusing on the wrong thing that you missed Me which means you missed the blessing.

I know many of you are wondering, how can Reverend Nobody address all of this, in this book. It is because I, Your Father, am speaking through Reverend Nobody, she is My Scribe to record what I, The Father am saying. The Father Who dictates the pre-ordained, The One Who gives the gifts, The Father Who does the calling and elevates, and it is I, The Father, Who created Reverend Nobody to be who she is and the Only One who can define where and how she serves in My Kingdom Building.

I sent my Son, Whom I entrusted to do His Father's Will, and I gave Him the power and authorities to bind, to heal, to deliver, to care for, to love others, and to speak with the authorities to anything in My Name. Likewise, I have entrusted My daughter, Reverend Nobody to do her Father's Will, and I gave her the power and the authorities to bind, to heal, to deliver, to care for, to love others, and to speak with the authorities to anything in My Name.

While treating Reverend Nobody in any deceptive way, know that you are treating Me in the same way. When you are gossiping about her, know that you are gossiping about Me. Know that when you are setting up plots with your acquaintances not to do what she may have asked, not attending those special prayer calls I put in place, the different workshops, the studying of My Words; Know that you were not being disobedient to Reverend Nobody, you were being disobedient to Me, The Father. For it is I, Your Father, Who told My daughter, the one Whom I send to be among you, and you have chosen not to be obedient. Like My Son Who cried out to me to forgive them for they do not know what they are doing. Likewise, I have heard the same cries coming from My daughter many times to whom many of you treated unkind to her, asking Me to forgive you for you do not know what you are doing. In the same way I have listened to My Son's cries, is the same way I have listened to My daughter's cries.

Many women in the Bible without names were overlooked in the midst of the calling I placed on their lives. They were overlooked for many reasons, some did not look wealthy or wear fine linens, and they were not from a royal line, in fact, some were living truly according to the world, but they too were My Ambassadors. Take, for example, the Gospel of John 4, "The Woman at the Well – The Samaritan Woman," the one whom many could not see beyond her faults. Not knowing why she was in the situations that she was in, they cast her out as one not even fit to be in their presence. Because of their unbelieving eyes, they could not see beyond her misfortunes. Yet through My Son, this woman without a name, was able to see herself to be One of My Ambassadors who did what her Father wanted of her. She accepted her position in Who I AM and became one of My Evangelists.

What about the woman who had been suffering from hemorrhaging for twelve years? The Gospel of Luke 8:43-48, talks about this woman, a no-name woman, only given the name the "Hemorrhaging Woman." One who was only seen by many to be unclean, not worthy to be in My presence or their presence. While this woman did not find favor in their eyes, I placed her in the right position to be recognized. She was so overlooked by the crowd, but she was able to get to My Son and touch the hem of His garment only to be healed by her faith. She refused to let their rejection keep her from her healing. Because of her faith on that day, because of her healing and her boldness, many came to Me. My child with no name stood on the Name of One whose name is above all names.

Many question the no-name woman in the epistles of 2 John, whom I have declared to be "The Chosen Lady." One to whom was not seen for her faithfulness to My truth. I, The Father chose My daughter to be "The Chosen Lady," for her holiness because she represented Me in caring for My people. Even though she was not given a name, and others were unkind towards her, My "Chosen Daughter" never fell prey to the temptations or responded in kind to the unkind treatments. I, The Father received glory through My "Chosen Lady" and her faithfulness towards her Father.

Although the many challenges My daughter, Reverend Nobody, and all of My daughters I have mentioned, went through, they never took their eyes off Me. It was I who allowed them to remain under the name of "Reverend Nobody, The chosen Lady, The woman with the blood". In those names, is it I who gets the glory. In those names, it is My Son's Name that each of My daughters stood on and relied on to keep them in the midst of their storms. I have chosen the ones without the "No Names" to be used by Me, The Father for the glory would be given to Me, and not you. Reverend Nobody and to the No Names who may not have fit in your plans, know that they are worthy and found great favor in Me, The Father, who knows the plans I had for them to fulfill.

"but those who hope in the Lord will renew their strength. They will soar on wings like eagles; they will run and not grow weary, they will walk and not be faint"

Isaiah 40:31

CHAPTER NINE

The Blessings

Blessings for Obedience
Deuteronomy 28:1-10

1 If you fully obey the Lord your God and carefully follow all his commands I give you today, the Lord your God will set you high above all the nations on earth. 2 All these blessings will come on you and accompany you if you obey the Lord your God: 3 You will be blessed in the city and blessed in the country. 4 The fruit of your womb will be blessed, and the crops of your land and the young of your livestock—the calves of your herds and the lambs of your flocks. 5 Your basket and your kneading trough will be blessed. 6 You will be blessed when you come in and blessed when you go out. 7 The Lord will grant that the enemies who rise up against you will be defeated before you. They will come at you from one direction but flee from you in seven. 8 The Lord will send a blessing on your barns and on everything you put your hand to. The Lord your God will bless you in the land he is giving you. 9 The Lord will establish you as his holy people, as he promised you on oath, if you keep the commands of the Lord your God and walk in obedience to him. 10 Then all the peoples on earth will see that you are called by the name of the Lord, and they will fear you.

I, Your Father, promised to the forefathers Abraham, Issac, and Jacob, the rewards to My children. It is a promise to the ones who are obedient to the plans of the Father.

You may ask why it is only for the ones who are obedient. My Commands that I have put in place are not to harm you but to give you, My children, the joy of being obedient to Your Father. My Commandments are there for My children to have a way to eternal rewards and blessings from Me, Your Father. My Commandments were given to Moses at Mount Sinai: Exodus 20:2-17 and Deuteronomy 5:6-21 which was a promise I made when I rescued My People from the hands of Pharoah.

You may be wondering why I, The Father, directed Reverend Nobody to speak on blessings. My blessings are not only to Reverend Nobody, or to a few people, but rather My blessings are for all of My children who are obedient to My Commandments and in following the Way, in which My Son laid out by the way He lived His life on earth. He laid the foundation.

While Reverend Nobody has experienced many challenges and disappointments by many, she has learned what it is to not only trust but to release everything to Me, The Father. The obedience of Reverend Nobody in the many challenges she had to face shows who she is in Me. Reverend Nobody did now allow her challenges to hold her back from surrendering to Me, even in those wildernesses she had to journey, she has never stopped being obedient the Me, The Father.

It is through Reverend Nobody's obedience that she has found great favor with her Father and because of that her children and her children's children will be blessed. My blessings are stored up for her lineage. When you are obedient to My Commandments you will be granted the rewards which I, Your Father have promised to you and your children's children. My Words in the Book of Deuteronomy 28:1-10 as stated above, sealed the rewards of the blessings from your obedience.

My strength is to be with all of My children and to grant them the blessings I, Your Father promises.

"Whatever you do, work at it with all your heart, as working for the Lord, not for human masters, since you know that you will receive an inheritance from the Lord as a reward. It is the Lord Christ you are serving"

COLOSSIANS 3:23-24

CONCLUSION
The Next Chapter

Giving full credit to Reverend Luther Barnes the composer and the Restoration Worship Center Choir on their album "The Favor of God." The words tell us of how much God's promises are secure and real to each of us whose names may or may not ever be mentioned or given the proper credit. Because of God's Grace and His Mercy kept me and you, the "No Names" to be and accomplish all that God has ordained and planned for us.

While on my journey as Reverend Nobody, I may never get the proper credits or acknowledgments throughout my journey but that is not why I do My Father's work, I do it because He is My Father and I love Him. I do it because I want to please Him. I do it because it is what He requires of all of us. I am secure and know that it is "The Favor of God," and His promises to me that have kept me. I continue to stand on My Father's Word in Jeremiah 1:5; "Before I formed you in the womb I knew you, before you were born I set you apart; I appointed you as a prophet to the nations" (NIV).

I thank Reverend Luther Barnes for God's guidance in the words of his song, "The Favor of God." If I could choose a theme song, it would be this song.

I encourage you, as you listen to the song during your quiet time, to allow the Holy Spirit to speak through the song. Know that while others may not see you beyond being the "No Name", that The Father has prepared you for your next chapter. In your next chapter know that you will never have to worry about who's going to validate you, for The Father has already done so.

The Father wants us the ones who are classified as the "No Names" to know that He has pre-destined us to be His Ambassadors for His Glory.

In your next chapter, never will you have to seek approval or seek to hear your name/s called for acknowledgment of the works you will be doing. For your approval already signed and sealed by Your, Father, the Ultimate Creator, who knows the plans He has for you.

It is in your next chapter, The Father will be using you the "No Name" to be His Messenger to His people. Where, The Father, will entrust you to watch over His people, to love, to care, to comfort His people.

Reverend Nobody, I had to understand that my validations did not come from the ones who thought they control me, to the ones who did not want to see beyond their own selfish ways but finds ways to take self-praises for the things The Father had Reverend Nobody to do. I had to learn while experiencing those wilderness encounters by those unkind and self-rewarding ones. I did not allow having a name given by them to pull or trap me in their selfless ways.

Reverend Nobody was not given a name that was bigger than they would ever imagine or thought of. Because it was bigger than the ones who could not see beyond their own ways, I find comfort in the Arms of The Father. So, I encourage you as you journey into your next chapter, trust Your, Father to guide you through those unkind words, and not accepting who you are. Know that the ones who are unkind to you, are truly dealing with their own selfish ways, and grief in the way they treated you. For Your Father, is not pleased in the ways of their selflessness of taking credit and mistreating towards the one He called, the one He has chosen to be His Ambassador.

ABOUT THE AUTHOR

REVEREND JOAN L. DAVIS

ABOUT ME

In 2013, when Joan accepted her calling as an Evangelist, little did she know the magnitude of the plans that God had for her life. Joan grew up in the church but would often say, "I was brought up in the church all my life, but after a while, the Church was not in me." Nonetheless, just like God told the prophet, Jeremiah, "Before I formed thee in the belly I knew thee, and before thou camest forth out of the womb I sanctified thee." God gave Joan just enough time to explore her options and to run from her calling, and in His perfect time, she yielded and surrendered to Him.

www.joanldavislifecoaching.com | info@joanldavislifecoaching.com

BONUS CONTENT

Today I'm grateful for...

IF YOU DON'T REMEMBER ANYTHING
ELSE, REMEMBER THIS...
GOD HAS NEVER TAKEN HIS EYES OFF
OF YOU AND HE NEVER WILL.

---

www.joanldavislifecoaching.com

Father, I am believing you for...

MY NOTES

GOD'S LOVE

God's love goes so far for you that He gave His only begotten son so that you may have everlasting life.

What is God saying to me today?

Date:

_____

_____

_____

_____

_____

_____

_____

_____

_____

_____

_____

_____

_____

_____

_____

_____

AS YOU PRAY, STAND ON GOD'S PROMISES

PRAYER REQUESTS

PRAYER REQUESTS

SCRIPTURES ON GOD'S PROMISES

SCRIPTURES ON GOD'S PROMISES

5 minute journaling

_____
_____
_____
_____
_____
_____
_____
_____
_____
_____
_____
_____
_____
_____
_____

Today I'm grateful for...

×

"No need to
make plans,
God already
made them.

Jeremiah 29:11

Father, I am believing you for...

MY NOTES

What is God saying to me today?

Date:

_____

_____

_____

_____

_____

_____

_____

_____

_____

_____

_____

_____

_____

_____

_____

_____

_____

_____

_____

Yes, God hears you.

Today I'm grateful for...

He is a way maker

"WHEN LIFE BEGINS
TO HAPPEN, GOD
SAYS DON'T WORRY,
I KNEW THIS WOULD
HAPPEN, I'VE
ALREADY MADE A
WAY."

AS YOU PRAY, STAND ON GOD'S PROMISES

PRAYER REQUESTS

PRAYER REQUESTS

SCRIPTURES ON GOD'S PROMISES

SCRIPTURES ON GOD'S PROMISES

Father, I am believing you for...

What is God saying to me today?

Date:

_____

_____

_____

_____

_____

_____

_____

_____

_____

_____

_____

_____

_____

_____

_____

_____

_____

_____

_____

_____

EVERY MORNING REMEMBER TO...

Rise &
SHINE

5 minute journaling

_____

_____

_____

_____

_____

_____

_____

_____

_____

_____

_____

_____

_____

_____

_____

_____

_____

AS YOU PRAY, STAND ON GOD'S PROMISES

PRAYER REQUESTS

PRAYER REQUESTS

SCRIPTURES ON GOD'S PROMISES

SCRIPTURES ON GOD'S PROMISES

MY NOTES

Father, I am believing you for...

He Restores
MY SOUL

What is God saying to me today?

Date:

_____

_____

_____

_____

_____

_____

_____

_____

_____

_____

_____

_____

_____

_____

_____

_____

_____

_____

Today I'm grateful for...

_____
_____
_____
_____
_____
_____
_____
_____
_____
_____
_____
_____
_____
_____
_____
_____
_____
_____
_____

Rev. Joan L. Davis

Motivational Speaker, Coach, Author & Group Facilitator

Reverend Joan is a highly rated motivational speaker with 8+ years of experience as a women's coach and group facilitator. Rev. Joan works with groups, individuals and organizations to amplify their authenticity and empower them to become a better version of themselves. Reverend Joan is founder of the Empowered For The Journey Toward Excellence Webinar.

SIGNATURE TOPICS

✓ Spiritual Breakthrough

✓ Women Empowerment

✓ Wellness and Self-care

✓ Managing Anxiety and Stress

✓ Being Your Authentic Self

✓ Prioritizing Mental Health in the Workplace

✓ Breathwork and Meditation

✓ Grief & Loss (Healing Process)

www.joanldavislifecoaching.com

info@joanldavislifecoaching.com

Stay Blessed

SOME OF MY COACHING PACKAGES

BREAKTHROUGH SESSION

- Goal Setting
- Preparing for an event or crucial conversation
- Dealing with indecision-making or self-sabotage
- Managing a crisis or conflict situation

MENTORSHIP

- Freedom
- Obstacles
- Reclaim Your Power

DISCIPLESHIP

- [Spiritual gifts/spiritual growth (Mind, Body, Soul)]

CLIENT FEEDBACK

"Reverend Joan is an amazing coach and a powerful source of support. Her dedication and commitment to my growth is undeniable. She continues to give me practical tools to use throughout my journey."

Lisa Taitt-Stevenson

Rev. Davis is caring and compassionate. She is committed to helping you get through the process of understanding your purpose in life and how to achieve the best that God has for you. She is a true gift to all who she encounters. My life has truly been enriched as she addresses the whole person, mind, body and soul.

Zina Porter

Please feel free to reach out for any questions.

Get in Touch!

✉ info@joanldavislifecoaching.com

🌐 www.joanldavislifecoaching.com

📞 484-882-3156